P9-CQT-479

This edition published by Parragon in 2012
Parragon
Queen Street House
4 Queen Street
Bath BA1 1HE, UK
www.parragon.com

ISBN 978-1-4454-8100-5

Printed in China

The Ugly Duckling

Retold by Sarah Delmege
Illustrated by Polona Lovsin

Parragon

It was a warm summer's day and Mommy Duck wriggled excitedly on her nest. She could hear a tapping noise. Tap, tap, tap, tap!

"Quick! Quack! Quick!"

Mommy Duck called to the other ducks.

"My eggs are hatching. Come and see!"

One by one, the eggs hatched and out popped six chirpy little ducklings.

Cheep!

Cheep!

Cheep!

Cheep!

Cheep!

Cheep!

“Ahhhh!” the other ducks sighed. “What sweet little ducklings!”

Mommy Duck beamed with pride.

But the biggest egg of all still hadn't opened. Mommy Duck was sure she had only laid six eggs ...

Craaaaaaaaaaaaaak!

Just then, the final egg burst open.

"Oh!" gasped Mommy Duck.

The last duckling wasn't little, yellow, or cute. He was enormous, gray and, well, ugly.

"What an ugly duckling!" quacked an old duck.

"He's not ugly!" said Mommy Duck protectively. "He's special."

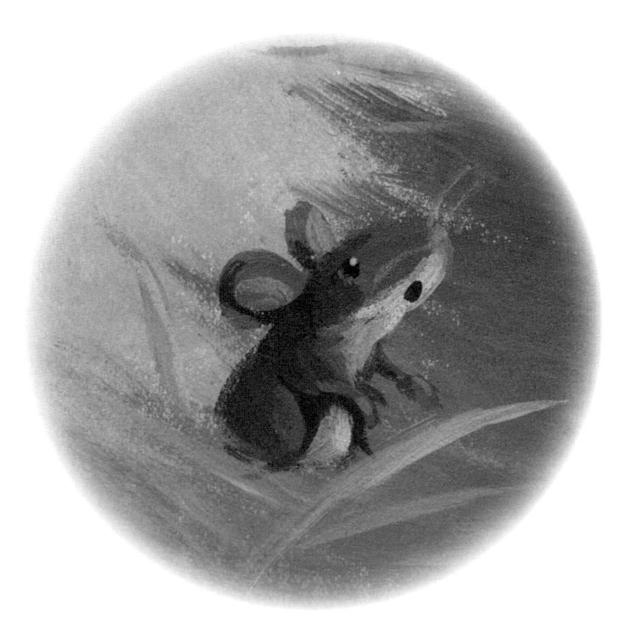

The next day, Mommy Duck took all her little ducks to the farmyard, to meet the other animals.

The six yellow ducklings proudly puffed out their pretty feathers.

"Ah," sighed the animals, "what lovely ducklings."

The ugly duckling waddled forward.

"Hello," he said quietly.

Everyone turned to stare at him.

"He's so GRAY!" neighed the horse.

"He's so CLUMSY!"

mooed the cow.

"He's so BIG!"

squawked the hen.

Large teardrops rolled down the ugly duckling's long, black beak. He felt all alone.

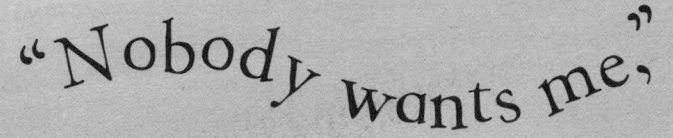

"Nobody wants me,"

he whispered. "I'd be better off swimming away."

The poor little duckling waddled sadly across the meadow, leaving the farm and his family far behind him.

Soon the ugly duckling came to a river, where some geese were diving for food.

"Excuse me," the ugly duckling began bravely, "have you seen any ducklings like me?"

"No. You're the strangest looking duckling we've ever seen," the geese honked.

So the ugly duckling kept waddling. He was getting very tired.

As darkness fell, he crept inside an old barn, looking for a place to rest.

"May I stay here?"

he asked the animals inside.

"Can you lay eggs?"

clucked a hen.

"No," said the ugly duckling sadly.

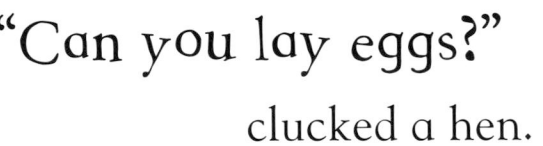

"Can you catch mice?" purred a cat.

"I don't think so," said the ugly duckling.

"Then you're no use here!"

the cat hissed.

The ugly duckling quickly waddled away. He kept going until he came to a large lake.

"If nobody wants me, then I'll just hide here forever," he sniffed sadly.

"Ribbit!" croaked a frog. "What a funny-looking duckling!"

Fall came and the leaves turned gold.

One evening, just as the sun was setting, the ugly duckling saw a flock of beautiful white birds flying gracefully across the sky.

"I wish I looked like them," he sighed.

All through the long winter, the ugly duckling hid in the reeds, ashamed to show his face.

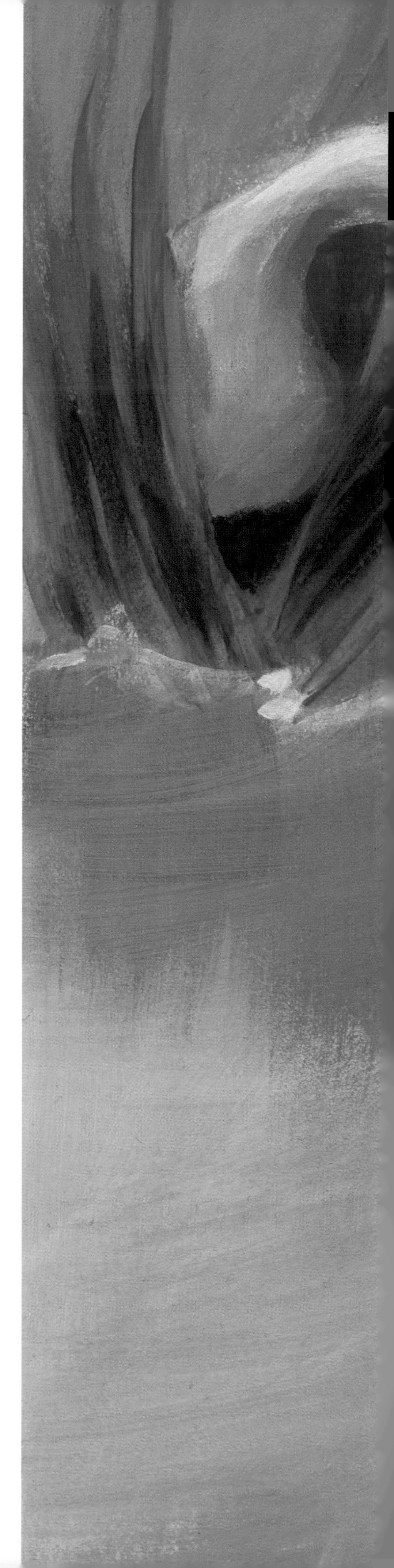

When the first rays of warm spring sunshine arrived, the ugly duckling peered out of his hiding place. A graceful swan paddled by him, and he backed away, afraid he would be teased.

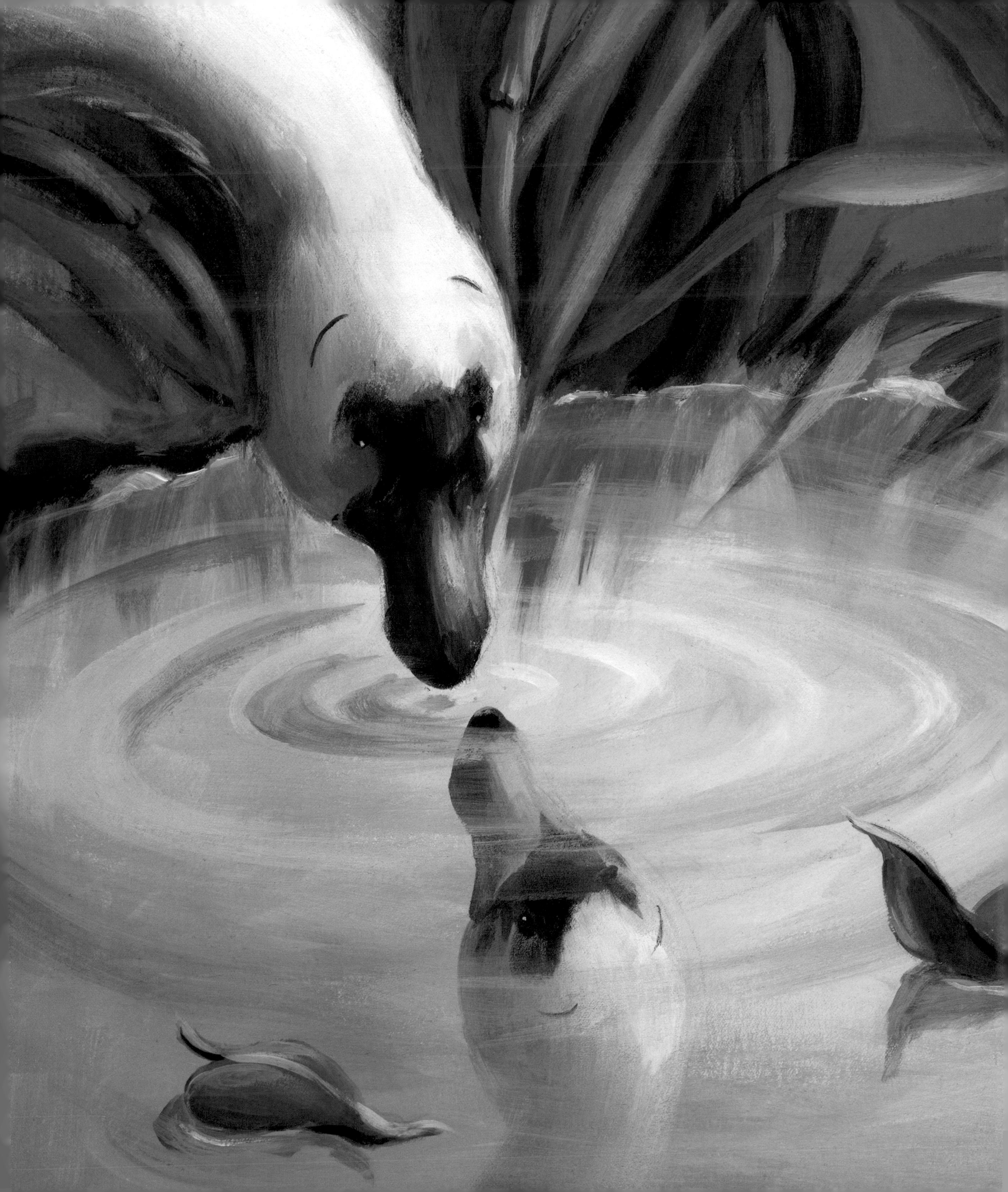

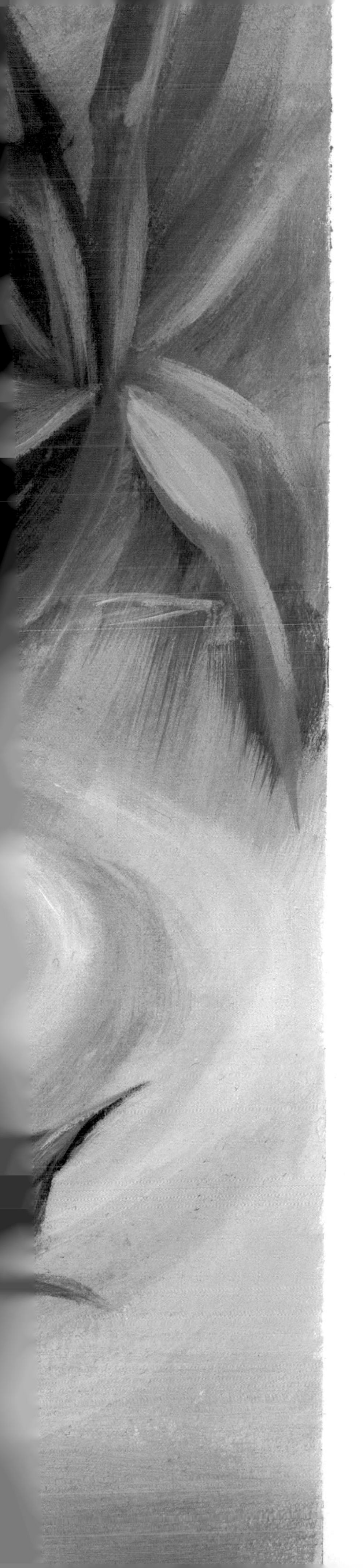

But to the ugly duckling's surprise, the swan swam up to him.

"Why are you hiding here?" asked the swan, kindly. "Join the rest of us."

The ugly duckling was shocked. Surely the swan must be talking to someone else.

But then he caught sight of his reflection in the lake.

He stared and gasped in amazement. His gray feathers were now snowy white!

"I'm a swan!" the ugly duckling cried happily.

Just then, a family of six young ducks waddled along the riverbank with their mother.

"Look at that beautiful swan!" they quacked.

Just then, a family of six young ducks waddled along the riverbank with their mother.

"Look at that beautiful swan!" they quacked.

But to the ugly duckling's surprise, the swan swam up to him.

"Why are you hiding here?" asked the swan, kindly. "Join the rest of us."

The ugly duckling was shocked. Surely the swan must be talking to someone else.

But then he caught sight of his reflection in the lake.

He stared and gasped in amazement. His gray feathers were now snowy white!

"I'm a swan!" the ugly duckling cried happily.

Mommy Duck recognized her little ugly duckling at once. "I always knew he was special," she quacked.

The ugly duckling ruffled his beautiful white feathers, turned away, and proudly paddled after his new friend.